MUMPS MANIA

A Run-Away Virus Tale

By Geraldine Ryan-Lush

Illustrations (c) Mulberry Animation

ISBN 978-1-989430-05-7

PUBLISHED BY MULBERRY BOOKS

Suggested Retail Price $16.95

MUMPS MANIA: A Run-Away Virus Tale is printed in Comic Sans MS

The Mumps! The Mumps!

I've got the Mumps!

They're in my face

In big red lumps

They swelled up BIG

They swelled up PINK

They glowed like PSYCH-E-DELIC INK!

They're in my face

They're here to stay

I cannot go to school today

I cannot, cannot leave this house

Or leave this room

Or leave this bed-

The Doctor came

He said, real slow:

"If you want those mumps to go....

YOU HAVE TO STAY IN BED YOU KNOW!!"

Stay in my bed?

Stay in my room?

Stay in this house

Of doom and gloom?

With two big lumps

Stuck in my jaws?

Why I could pass

As Santa Claus!

A giant chipmunk too I look

From one of sister's nursery books!

Stay in this bed?

Stay in this room?

Stay in this house

Of doom and gloom?

YOU   HAVE   TO   BE   KIDDING!

So just as Doctor's out the door

My feet are landing on the floor

My feet are landing on the walk-

I cannot yell

I cannot talk-

With two big lumps

Stuck in my jaws

The MAILMAN thinks

I'm Santa Claus!

My feet are landing

On the road

I feel just like

An ugly toad

With two big lumps

Stuck in my chops

I look just like

Tricerotops!

I cannot talk

I cannot scream

Now don't you think

That's kind of mean?

With two big lumps

Stuck in my jaws

My Nanny thinks

I'm Santa Claus!

Up and down

And through the town

A HELMET on

my burning crown!

The Doctor came

He seemed perturbed:

"Why, this is strange...

 it's most absurd....

He felt my mumps

Those GIANT ROCKS

Those lumpy lumps

Of STICKY LOCKS!

He felt around

And sighed, and said:

"If you want those

mumps to go-

(Real patient-like

and slow)-

YOU   HAVE   TO STAY

IN BED YOU KNOW!!

Stay in my bed?

Stay in my room?

Stay in this house

Of doom and gloom?

With two big lumps

Stuck in my jaws

My Parrott thinks

I'm Santa Claus!

A giant chipmunk too I look

From one of sister's

nursery books!

Stay in my bed?

Stay in this room?

Stay in this house?

Of doom and gloom?!

YOU HAVE TO BE KIDDING!

So just as Doctor's

down the stairs

My feet are on

A DOZEN CHAIRS-

My feet are on

The WINDOW WIDE

A DOZEN SHEETS before me

Tied!

My feet are landing in

THE DARK!

It looks just like

JURASSIC PARK!

I cannot yell

I cannot scream

Now don't you think that's

Kind of MEAN?

With two big lumps

Stuck in my face

I LOOK LIKE SOMETHING

OUT OF SPACE!

(I'M NOT FIT FOR THE HUMAN RACE!)

With two big lumps

Stuck in my mug

I look just like

A WATER JUG!

Up and Down

And

through the Town

A ZOMBIE with a

BURNING CROWN!

The Doctor came

He scratched his hair

"Those mumps, those bumps

ARE STILL THERE??!!

He authorized a RED MACHINE

And MEDICAL INTERNS

All SIXTEEN

Then called for TWENTY GUYS

IN WHITE-

From T.V. and from TEN

WEBSITES!-

To spread the word

about my FATE

It had become an

awful STATE!

It was so STRANGE

So MUMPSTER-IF-IC-

So FANT-AB-U-LOUSLY

SCIENTIFIC!

They spread the WORD

They spread it FAR!

BREAKING
NEWS

BREAKING NEWS

Prime Minister saw it in

His Car!

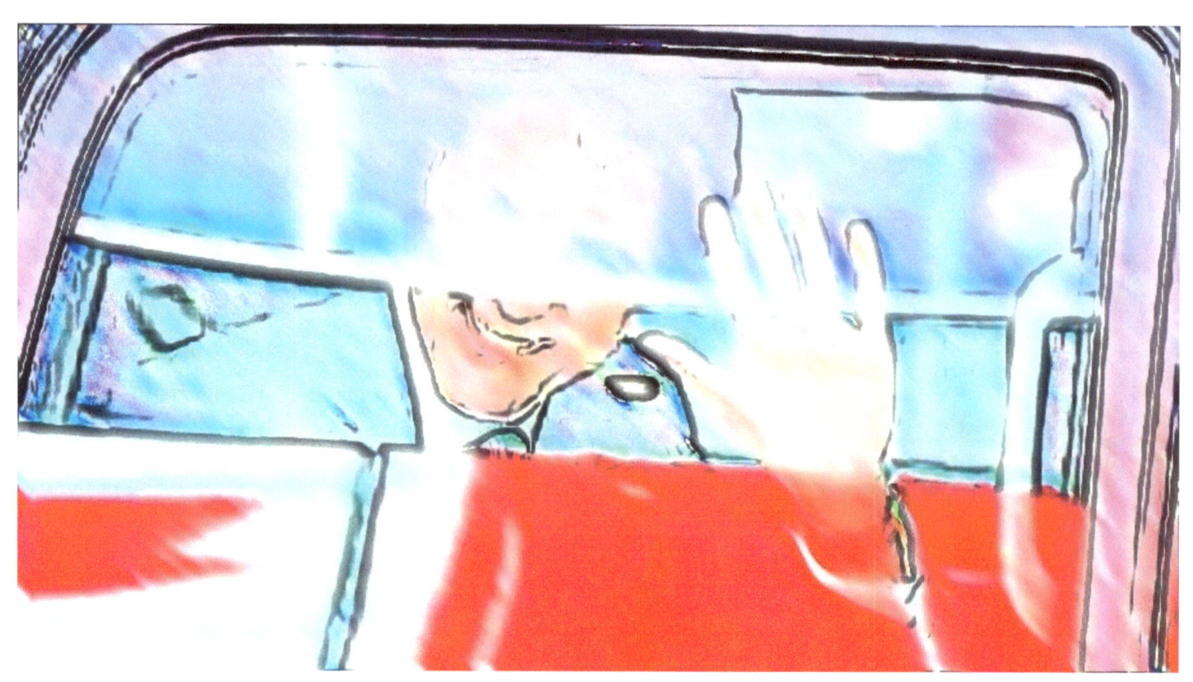

Those TWENTY MILLION

PRESS RELEASES

Of AUTOGRAPHED

And PHOTOGRAPHED

And LITHOGRAPHED

DISEASES!!

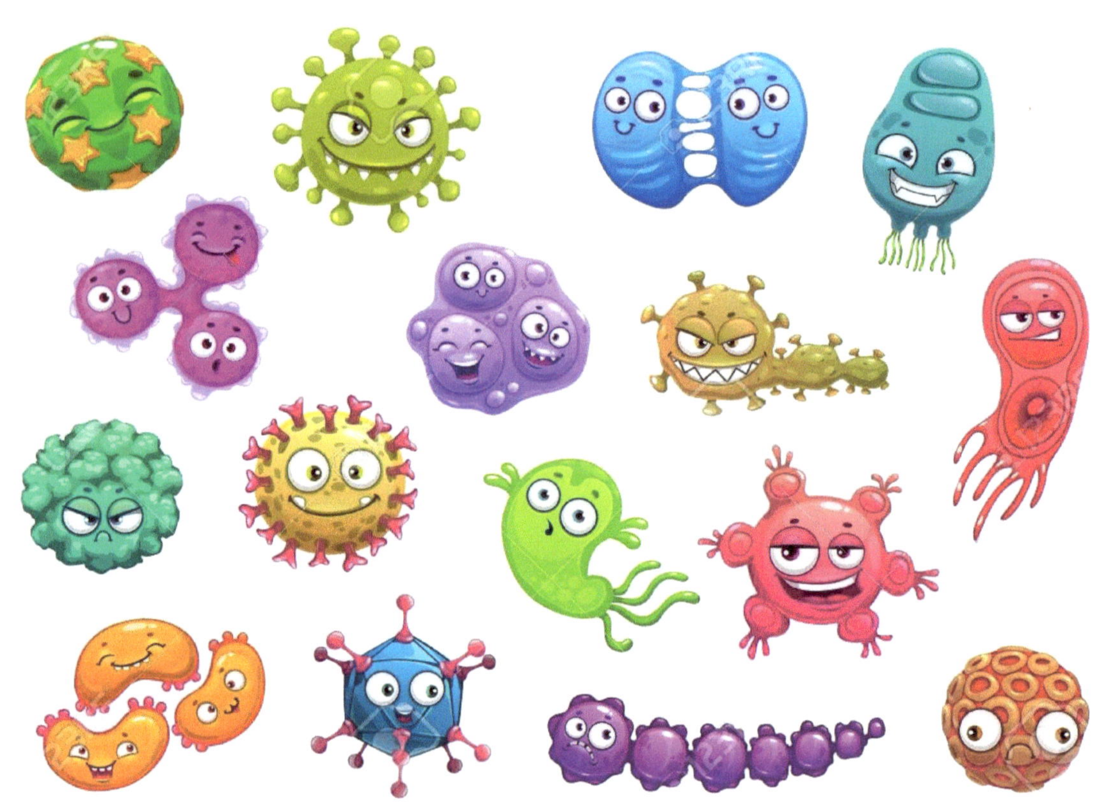

My parents came

They fixed my bed

They felt my lumps

They kissed my head

My Mom said sternly

And real slow-

"If you want those

mumps to go-

YOU HAVE TO STAY IN   BED

YOU KNOW!"

Stay in my bed?

Stay in this room?

Stay in this house

Of DOOM and GLOOM?

With two big lumps

In my PHYSOGUE

I look just like

A LUMPY LOG!

With two big lumps

stuck in my jaws

My GOLDFISH think

I'm Santa Claus!

A GIANT CHIPMUNK

Too I look

From one of sister's

Nursery books!

Stay in my bed?

Stay in this room?

Stay in this house

Of DOOM and GLOOM?

YOU   HAVE   TO   BE

KIDDING!

So just as Mother's

down the hall

My feet are landing

on the wall-

My feet are landing

In the bushes

With SLIMY SNAKES

And BLACK BULRUSHES!

I cannot yell

I cannot scream

Now don't you think

That's kind of mean?

With two big lumps

Stuck in my jaws

The GOPHERS think

I'm Santa Claus!

The Doctor came

He tore his hair

"Those MUMPS

Those BUMPS

ARE STILL THERE??!!

He rolled his eyes

His face turned green

"We have to try a new machine."

He turned a crank

He pressed a bell

He stuck it on

A lump that swelled

But nothing happened

Not at all-

The mumps

Are still like

BOWLING BALLS

My parents came

They fixed my bed-

They felt my lumps

They kissed my head-

They phoned their lawyer

And their friends:

"We have a message

 We must send:

 THAT DOCTOR WITH THE RED

 MACHINE

 AND MEDICAL INTERNS ALL SIXTEEN

 HE'S NOT ALLOWED

 TO COME TODAY

  HE DID NOT TAKE THOSE MUMPS

  AWAY."

It was an overnight sensation

The Doctor's in

COMPLETE FRUSTRATION

CONSTERNATION

HIBERNATION

And ETERNAL LITIGATION!

BREAKING
NEWS

My friends all skyped

To see my face-

It was a MESS-

A REAL DISGRACE!

To have those mumps

So long, you see-

A MEDICAL CAT-AS-ROPHE-E!

The teacher called

She was concerned:

"What's this, What's this

That I have learned?!

Those *lumps,* those *bumps*

mumps you call them

In the Square-

YOU STILL HAVE THEM?

THEY'RE STILL THERE???!!!

I said "Yes, Miss-

Yes, I do-

I still have them

C'est flambeau!"

"Don't think you

Can be in the Fair-

You may become

A REAL HEALTH SCARE!"

She said Goodbye so dignified

But wholly, totally MORTIFIED!

I thought about the things

she said-

This time I did

STAY IN MY BED!

I missed my friends

I missed the FAIR-

I did not want a

REAL HEALTH SCARE!

Stay in my bed?

Stay in my room?

Stay in this house

Of DOOM and GLOOM?

With two big lumps

That are swollen pink-

But WAIT! I THINK

THEY'RE STARTING

TO SHRINK!!!

My parents came

They fixed my bed

They felt my lumps

They kissed my head-

They phoned their lawyer

And their friends:

"We have a message we must send:

  THAT DOCTOR WITH

  THE RED MACHINE

  AND MEDICAL INTERNS

  ALL SIXTEEN

  HE IS ALLOWED

  TO COME TODAY

  THE MUMPS HAVE GONE

  THEY'VE GONE AWAY!

The news completely

Shook the Nation

A BLITZ, A MEDIA SENSATION!

The Doctor's out of HIBERNATION

FRUSTRATION

CONSTERNATION

And ETERNAL LITIGATION!

PRESCRIPTION

PAPARAZZI

And strange machines that turn

And crank-

But wait!

Another little prank....

For just as I

took off my socks

There were hundreds little

Tiny spots..

I THINK I'VE GOT

THE CHICKEN POX!

BUT NOW I KNOW JUST

WHAT TO DO-

DO YOU??

THE END

MiSS
YOU

About The Author

Geraldine Ryan-Lush holds a B.A. (ED) from Memorial University of Newfoundland, majoring in English Language and Literature. Prior to her writing career, she was a classroom teacher, and print columnist for The Evening Telgram and Newfoundland Herald. She is the prolific and multi-award-winning author of 18 books, ranging from picture books to junior novels, to young adult and adult. She is also a celebrated poet, with a collection of adult poetry to her credit, as well as 4 rhyming children's books. She is also author of numerous scholarly articles on the children's literature field, published in sources as Books In Canada, Canadian Children's Literature, and The NL Quarterly. Her books, some in French translation, have been reviewed in prestigious sources as School Library Journal, New York, Canadian Book Review Annual, Canadian Children's Literature, Quill & Quire, The Toronto Star, Copley News Services, Washington, D.C., London Free Press, The Observer, Montreal, Winnipeg Free Press, Canadian Materials, and a plethora of other sources in the literary and popular stance. Her Awards and Honours for her books include American Bookseller's Pick Of The Lists, Merit Magazine Studio Award, Alcuin Society Design Award, Readers' Favourite 5-Star (A review source honored by the American Library Association), twice, Atlantic Books Today Editors' Pick, Major Canada Council for the Arts Grant, and Major Newfoundland Arts Council Grant awarded for her Malcolm K. Wall series of junior novels for ages 7-12. She is also 3-times Winner of the Canada Book Award, for her young adult novel, "The Gravel Pit Kids," her adult novel "Seashell's Lament," and her folklore-themed rhyming tale "Goodbye Wart!" Geraldine has two grown sons, Shannon and Barrie, daughter-in-law Stephanie, granddaughters Lyla and Riley, grand fur babies Smokey and Scooby-Doo. Born and raised in St. Joseph's, Newfoundland, she resides in Mount Pearl, NL, Canada.

Books by Geraldine Ryan-Lush:

- *The Gravel Pit Kids* (Young Adult Novel, Black Rose Writing, 2017. Mulberry Books 2020)

- *Mumps Mania: A Run-Away Virus Tale* (Mulberry Books 2020) All

Ages Appeal)

-Haunted Towns: Ghost Stories Of Newfoundland & Labrador. Non-Fiction Collection). Mulberry Books 2019

-*Seashell's Lament* (Contemporary Adult Novel. Black Rose Writing 2016. Mulberry Books 2020)

-*Mrs. Clohiggledy's Clutter* (Picture Story Book. Written and illustrated by Geraldine Ryan-Lush. All Ages Appeal. Mulberry Books 2015)

-*The Law-Breaking Adventures Of Teacher Tabitha* (Junior Novel. Mulberry Books 2018)

-*Hannigan's Hand* (Paranormal Novel. Adult. Mulberry Books 2013)

-*Hannigan's Hand: The Ghost Woman Talks* (Paranormal Novel. Adult. Mulberry Books 2015)

-*Malcolm The Klutz* (Junior Novel, Malcolm K. Wall Series, Mulberry Books 1998)

-*Malcolm And The Hamster Lady* (Junior Novel, Malcolm K. Wall Series. Mulberry Books 2003)

-No Go Potty! (Junior Novel, Malcolm K.Wall Series. Mulberry Books 2015)

-*Once When I Wasn't Looking* (Poetry Collection. Borealis Press 2007)

-*Hairs On Bears* (Picture Book. Annick Press. 1994. Illustrated by Normand Cousineau)

-Poils Poils Et Repoils (Picture Book. Annick Press. 1994)

-Jeremy Jeckles Hates Freckles (Junior Novel. Breakwater Books 1992. Illustrated by Kathy Kaulbach)

-Goodbye Wart! (Picture Book. Written by Geraldine Ryan-Lush. Illustrated by Geraldine Ryan-Lush and Doriano Strologo)

-Haunted Towns, Volume Two. (Non-Fiction Collection. Mulberry Books 2020)

Contact: Facebook: AuthorGeraldineRyanLush

Twitter: @GRyanLush   geraldine1942@live.com

To Purchase:

Mulberry Books, 28-A Ewing's Road, CBS, NL. Canada A1A4H3

www.mulberrybooks.com   www.amazon.ca   www.amazon.com
www.chapters.indigo.ca   www.barnes&noble.com
www.walmart.com   www.waterstones.uk